To

From

With thanks to Jane Horne.

This edition first published in 2010 by Castle Street Press
an imprint of make believe ideas ltd.

Copyright © 2008

make believe ideas ltd.

27 Castle Street, Berkhamsted,
Hertfordshire, HP4 2DW.
565, Royal Parkway, Nashville, TN 37214, USA.

Manufactured in China

DUCKIE DUCK

KATE TOMS

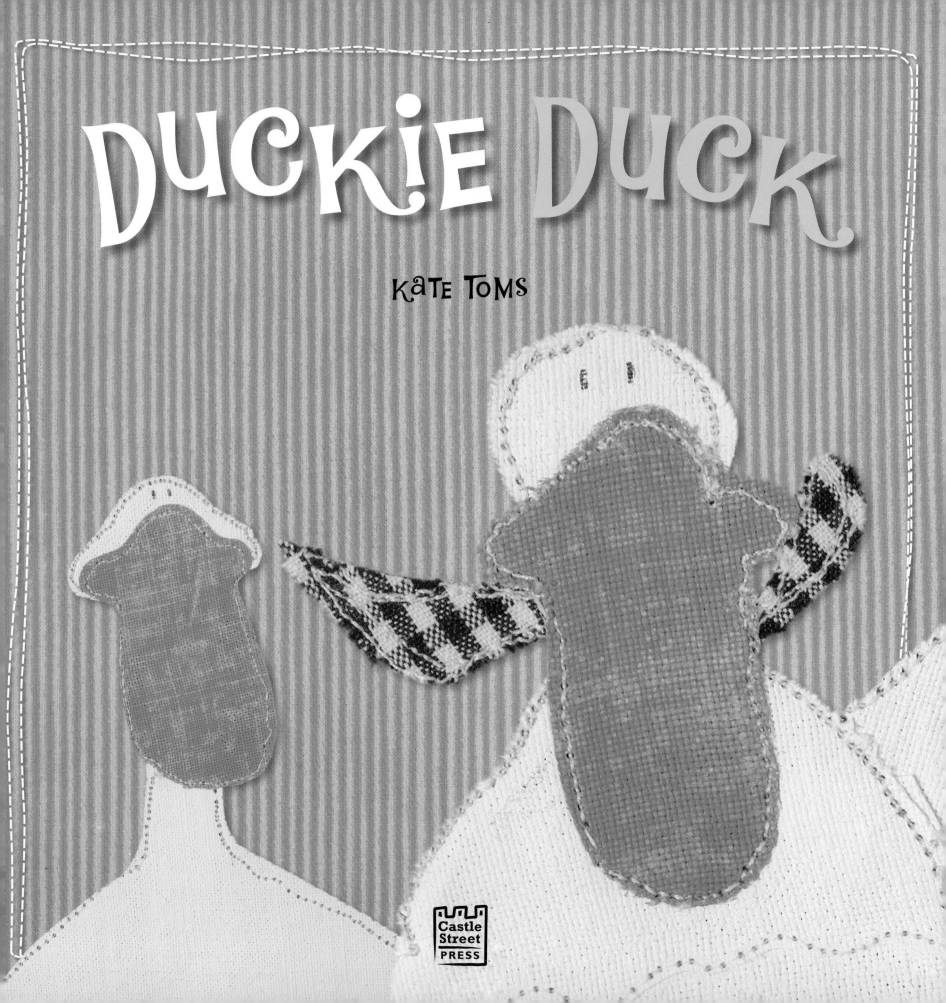

Castle Street PRESS

but Duckie whistles a happy song.

The other little ducks
all love to swim

but not Duckie—
a boat is best
for him!

Ducks all waddle
when they go
to the shop.

The ducks
eat grass
at dinnertime.

Duckie thinks
a picnic
will be just fine!

In a frenzy of flapping, ducks take to the sky.

while
Duckie's
balloon

floats
quietly
by.

Feathers fly when
the ducks spy a fox...

but Duckie
stands firm,
as strong as an ox!

The ducks hurry home when day turns to night . . .

but
Duckie goes out
with a bright
flashlight!

At night,
the ducks gather
in the warmth of
their shed,

ZZZZ ZZZZ
ZZZZ ZZZ
ZZZZ
ZZZ

while Duckie goes
exploring in his sporty
little car.

Heads in the water,

1, 2, 3!

Quack

Quack

Quack

Duckie says, "NO! That's not for me!"

but for **Duckie**, being different is what he likes best!